This book is dedicated to the memory of our parents,
Frank J. and Mary A. Hoffelt.
They taught their five daughters how to share
one house in peace.

Jane E. Hoffelt & Marty Husted

About the Endpapers

The world map shown at the beginning and ending of this book is based on the Dymaxion Map™ created in 1938 by R. Buckminster Fuller—a remarkable mathematician, educator, inventor, humanitarian and visionary. This unique map of Earth's entire surface is visually undistorted, revealing our planet as "one big island in one big ocean." Fuller hoped that, given a way to see the whole planet with greater accuracy, we humans could better address the challenges we face aboard "Spaceship Earth."

Committed to helping us optimize our options, the Buckminster Fuller Institute carries on Fuller's legacy by educating and empowering people around the world. For more information visit www.bfi.org.

We Share One World

By Jane E. Hoffelt

Illustrated by Marty Husted

ILLUMINATION
Arts

Publishing Company, Inc.
Bellevue, Washington

You and I, we share one world,

Tanzania

One golden sun,

Switzerland

One silver moon.

Algeria

Day and night we breathe the air.

Japan

We touch the wind

And play our songs.

By the shore we hear the waves.

Iraq

We smell the rain.

Russia

We taste the snow.

Costa Rica

In the woods we laugh and play.

Canada

We find new paths

Australia

And make new friends.

You and I can dream one dream.

We share one world—

Let's live in peace.

ILLUMINATION
Arts

Publishing Company, Inc.
P.O. Box 1865, Bellevue, WA 98009
Tel: 425-644-7185 ✤ 888-210-8216 (orders only) ✤ Fax: 425-644-9274
liteinfo@illumin.com ✤ www.illumin.com

Library of Congress Cataloging-in-Publication Data

Hoffelt, Jane E., 1955-
    We share one world / by Jane E. Hoffelt ; illustrated by Marty Husted.
       p. cm.
    Summary: A young boy dreams of world peace as he realizes that people everywhere are
really the same.
    ISBN 0-9701907-8-6
       [1. Nature–Fiction. 2. Peace–Fiction.] I. Husted, Marty, 1957- ill. II. Title.

PZ7.H6728We 2004
[E]–dc22

                                                                                    2003062077

Second Printing 2006
Published in the United States of America
Printed in Singapore by Tien Wah Press Ltd.
Book Designer: Molly Murrah, Murrah & Company, Kirkland, WA

Illumination Arts is a member of Publishers in Partnership—replanting our nation's forests.

More inspiring picture books from Illumination Arts

Little Yellow Pear Tomatoes
Demian Elainé Yumei/Nicole Tamarin, ISBN 0-9740190-2-X
Ponder the never-ending circle of life through the eyes of a young girl, who marvels at all the energy and collaboration it takes to grow yellow pear tomatoes.

Something Special
Terri Cohlene/Doug Keith, ISBN 0-9740190-1-1
A curious little frog finds a mysterious gift outside his home near the castle moat. It's *Something Special*…What can it be?

Am I a Color Too?
Heidi Cole/Nancy Vogl/Gerald Purnell, ISBN 0-9740190-5-4
A young interracial boy wonders why people are labeled by the color of their skin. Seeing that people dream, feel, sing, dance and love regardless of their color, he asks, "Am I a color, too?"

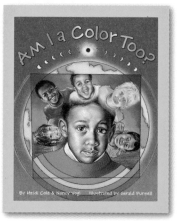

The Tree
Dana Lyons/David Danioth, ISBN 0-9701907-1-9
An urgent call to preserve our fragile environment, *The Tree* reminds us that hope for a brighter future lies in our own hands.

Too Many Murkles
Heidi Charissa Schmidt/Mary Gregg Byrne, ISBN 0-9701907-7-8
Each spring the people of Summerville gather to prevent the dreaded Murkles from entering their village. Unfortunately, this year there are more of the strange, smelly creatures than ever.

Your Father Forever
Travis Griffith/Raquel Abreu, ISBN 0-9740190-3-8

A devoted father promises to nurture, guide, protect and respect his beloved children. This heartwarming poem transcends the boundaries of culture and time in expressing a parent's universal love.

In Every Moon There Is A Face
Charles Mathes/Arlene Graston, ISBN 0-9701907-4-3
On this magical voyage of discovery and delight, children of all ages connect with their deepest creative selves.

A Mother's Promise
Lisa Humphrey/David Danioth ISBN 0-9701907-9-4
A lifetime of sharing begins with the sacred vow a woman makes to her unborn child.

To view our whole collection visit us at www.illumin.com

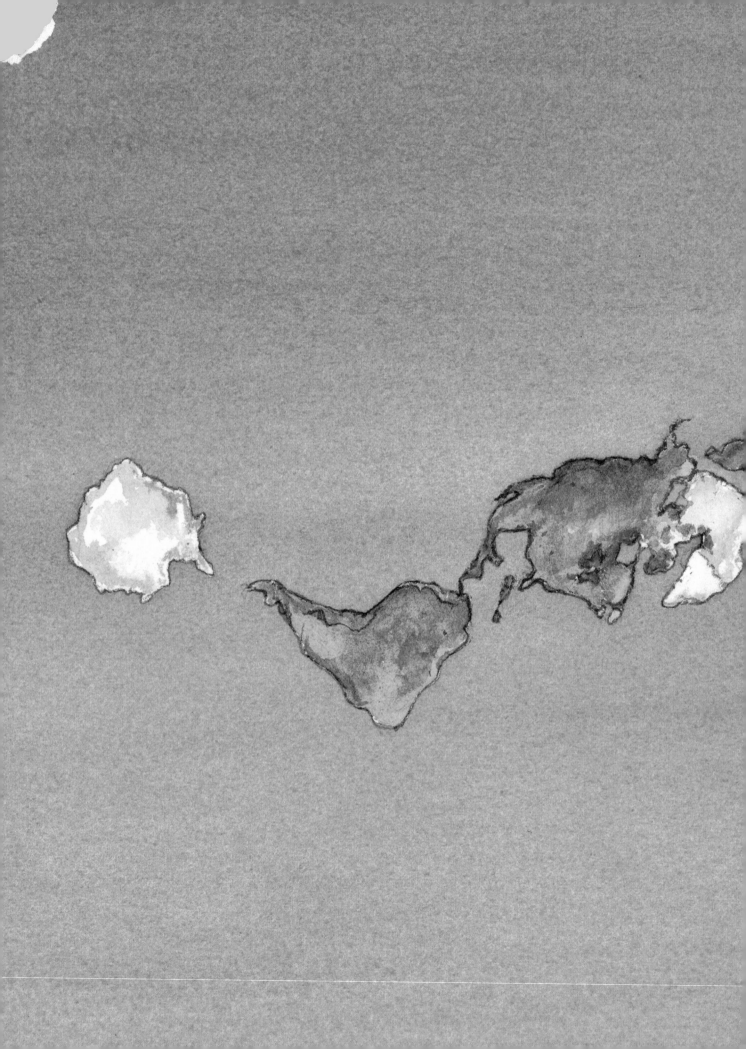